..·❦❧ TOM PERCIVAL ❦❧·..

Little Legends

THE SECRET MOUNTAIN

Tom Percival grew up in a remote and beautiful part of south Shropshire. It was so remote that he lived in a small caravan without mains electricity or any sensible form of heating. He thinks he's probably one of the few people in his peer group to have learned to read by gas lamp.

Having established ... illustrator, Little ... career as a picture-book ... first chapter-book series ... readers. The idea for Little ... gends was developed by Tom with Made in Me, a digital studio exploring new ways for technology and storytelling to inspire the next generation ...

... OKS

This book is dedicated to
Rory Pennington (and Icicles)

First published 2017 by Macmillan Children's Books
an imprint of Pan Macmillan
20 New Wharf Road, London N1 9RR
Associated companies throughout the world
www.panmacmillan.com

ISBN 978-1-5098-4215-5

Contents

1

*J*ack's foot slipped as he scrambled up the Story Tree which grew at the centre of Tale Town. Some trees are incredibly big, some are especially old, but the Story Tree was special in a different way. Every time a story was told near it, a new shoot would grow. A small story might grow into one leaf, but a long exciting story could turn into a whole branch covered in leaves.

1

If you ran your finger along the branch, the story would happen *inside your head*. It was an amazing thing to experience and the reason Tale Town had first got its name.

'It's *got* to be somewhere up here,' Jack muttered.

'**WhAaaat?**' squawked Betsy, Jack's magical talking hen. The only word Betsy could actually say was 'what', but even so, Jack and his friends always knew what she meant.

'You know, the story about the adventure we had last night?' Jack replied. 'When we were trapped on that boat, and the captain, who was a dog, was sailing us towards an island made out of bones?'

'WHAAAAAT!?' Betsy rolled her eyes.

'Of course it wasn't a *dream*!' insisted Jack. 'Anyway . . . when we got to the island it turned into a giant cake, and then . . .'

'Whaaaat?' clucked Betsy doubtfully.

Jack stopped climbing. 'OK. Maybe last night's adventure *was* a dream. But I'm sure other stories have been going missing from the Story Tree.

Like the one about when Anansi first arrived here. You remember . . . I thought that he was a troll spy because his uncle and mum are cursed to look like trolls, and I stole all those spells and, you know. . . I wasn't very nice . . .' he trailed off, embarrassed.

'Whaaat!' Betsy nodded. She knew that story *very* well.

'Well it's *gone*!' said Jack dramatically. 'And a whole load more as well!'

'WhAaaat?'

'Of *course* I'm looking in the right place, but all that's here is a freshly cut branch.'

'Hey, Jack!' came a voice from below them.

Jack peered down to see his friends Red, Anansi and Rapunzel, as well as Ella and Cole, her Fairy Godbrother.

'Hey, guys!' called Jack. 'Listen, I was just telling Betsy that stories are going missing from the Story Tree.'

'No way!' exclaimed Red.

'*Yes* way!' replied Jack.

'Are you sure?' asked Rapunzel.

Jack sighed. 'Come up and have a look for yourself if you don't believe me.'

It wasn't long before everyone was perched on different branches.

'Jack's right!' said Ella. 'I can't find the story about how Cole and I first met you all when we rescued Anansi's mum from that evil witch.'

'Awww!' complained Cole. 'That was the only one with me in!'

'I doubt it's anything personal,' said Red, smiling at Cole. 'But what I don't understand is *how* these stories have gone missing. The spell of protection on the Story Tree means that the only way to trim off a story is using the Sacred Shiny Story-Snipping Shears, and Mayor Fitch only ever does that once a year. Plus, it's usually the oldest stories that get taken off and stored to stop the Story

Tree getting overgrown. *These* missing stories are really recent . . .'

'*And* they're all about us!' muttered Rapunzel angrily. 'The story where I was cursed by a genie is gone too.'

'Fitch is up to something,' said Anansi. 'He must have been trimming stories off in secret – but why?'

'I don't know?' said Jack. 'But I'll *bet* he's up to no good.'

'**WhaAaaaaaaaat!**' squawked Betsy, her beady eyes flashing angrily.

'*Betsy!*' gasped Jack.

'**Whaaaaaaaaat...**' added Betsy quietly.

'I don't like Mayor Fitch *either*,' protested Jack. 'But *please*, mind your language! Anyway, at least we've still got our secret cutting from the Story Tree down in Lily's underwater cave. There's no way Fitch could have got to *that*.'

'Perhaps we should go and check it ...' began Ella, but she was distracted by a loud commotion. Several of Mayor Fitch's armed guards were dragging someone into the town square.

The group watched silently from up in the Story Tree as a small, hooded figure was dragged over to the ancient wooden stocks in the middle of the square, kicking and struggling.

Sometimes Jack and his friends would pretend to be locked in the stocks, but only for fun – none of them thought they were ever actually *used*.

'See how you like *that*!' barked one of Mayor Fitch's guards as she roughly secured the prisoner's small wrists, making the hooded figure cry out.

'Let's see if Mummy and Daddy come to get you!' added another with a mean grin. 'If they do . . . we'll be waiting!'

A third guard yanked the hood off

the prisoner's head and then they all turned and walked away. Jack looked over at Red; her eyes were wide with shock. Locked up in the stocks below them was a child.

A troll child.

2

'**D**id you *see* that?' whispered Jack from up in the branches of the tree.

'See what?' asked Rapunzel.

'Fitch's guards locking up the . . .' He paused as he noticed Rapunzel rolling her eyes. 'Oh, right,' he added. 'You *did* see.'

'What are we going to do?' asked Anansi. 'I mean, I know everyone says

Trolls mean Trouble, but he's only a child. He can't be older than us!'

'I can't believe they actually use those stocks,' said Ella. 'It's *totally* mean!'

'Do you think we should get him some water or something?' asked Cole, flitting around the Story Tree nervously. 'I'd hate it, being locked up like that – I mean, I know the wicked witch kept me and Ella locked up in her castle, but at least we could move about, and there was always water to drink – even if it *was* dripping down the walls of the room we slept in . . .'

'You're right!' said Red. 'We've got to do *something* – but what?'

'WHAAAAAAAAT!?!' squawked Betsy, as quietly as she could.

'That's a good idea, Betsy . . .' said Red. 'But if we *did* find a dragon, there's no guarantee that it wouldn't eat everyone here and then set fire to the whole town instead of just scaring the guards into setting him free.'

'WHAAAAAT!?' suggested Betsy.

Anansi shook his head. 'Even if we *could* invent a machine to freeze time and unlock him before the guards saw us – I don't know where we'd be able to find the equipment to make one.'

Betsy flapped angrily and squawked **'WhAaaat?'** once more.

'A secret meeting with the rest of the gang at the tree house in my garden?' exclaimed Red. 'Brilliant, Betsy! I'm sure someone will come up with a good idea.'

'Whaaat' muttered Betsy crossly.

Everyone scrambled down from the Story Tree and slipped out of the town square, taking worried looks back at the small troll prisoner. Jack asked Betsy to go and find Hansel, Gretel and as many of their other friends as she could, which she did, but she was still in a bad mood, so she did it a bit grumpily.

Red, Jack, Anansi, Ella, Cole and Rapunzel were running through town towards Red's house when a voice rang out that sent shivers down their spines. Well . . . the voice didn't so much 'ring out' as wheeze unpleasantly.

'Now, now, Miss Red!' called the seafood-snack salesman, Old Bert, as he pushed his wooden cart along the dusty street. 'What's the 'urry?'

'Oh, er, nothing . . . we were just . . .' Red looked around to see if any of her friends could help her out, but they all seemed to have vanished. Then she spotted Jack, who had wrapped himself in a nightie that was hanging up to dry on a washing line, and Anansi, who had climbed up a spider's web to hide underneath a dusty rooftop. Cole had *somehow* managed to turn

himself,
Ella and
Rapunzel
into hamsters.
His fairy
magic never
really worked
properly . . .

He'd probably been trying to make them invisible.

Red sighed. 'Listen, Bert,' she said firmly. 'I'm not buying *any* of your seafood snacks, OK? I don't like seafood, I never have and I *never* will!'

'Oh, I ain't sellin' that stuff any more,' said Bert, wrinkling his nose. 'No, I'm out of the snack game *for good*.'

'Then what's in your cart?' asked

Red suspiciously as the three hamsters scuttled around her feet.

'Stationery.'

'Stationery? Really?' Red loved drawing, and the one thing that she couldn't resist was a notebook or new set of pens.

'Fancy a look?' asked Old Bert, grinning his gap-toothed grin.

'Go on then,' replied Red, lifting up the lid of the cart. Even though the word 'Snacks' had been painted over and replaced with the word 'Stationary', it smelt just as fishy as it always had done.

Red wrinkled her nose. 'Er, Bert . . .' she said. 'Firstly that's not how you spell "stationery", and secondly, this *isn't* stationery – your cart's *still* filled with stinky old fish!'

'It ain't!' barked Bert, pulling out a large swordfish. 'Look, 'ere's a pencil.'

'That's a *swordfish*,' protested Red, 'with a grey bit painted on the end of its nose to make it look like a pencil.'

'Rubbish!' replied Bert, looking offended. He pulled out a flattened piece of dried seaweed, picked up the swordfish and started trying to write his name, but nothing happened.

'Stupid pencil . . .' muttered Bert. 'Must've run out of ink.'

Red grinned. 'Now I really have seen everything.'

'Oh, *really*?' asked Bert crossly, spinning around to face her. 'You ever seen a rat on a ship so hungry it'll eat itself? It starts with its tail . . .'

Red's eyes went wide and she shook her head.

'Then you haven't seen *everything*, have you?' said Bert triumphantly. 'Now if you don't mind, I'm a busy man.' He turned and hobbled off, pushing his squeaky old cart in front of him.

'It's OK – he's gone now!' Red called out as Bert walked away. One by one, her friends came out of hiding – apart from Cole, Ella and Rapunzel who were still hamsters.

'I can't work out how to undo the spell,' squeaked the hamster with blue fur that must have been Cole. 'Sorry . . .'

'Typical!' squeaked a hamster with long, blonde plaits.

'Don't worry. I'm sure Cole will work it out,' replied the third hamster,

who was worriedly inspecting a small
hole in the toe of one of Red's shoes.

'Let's sort it out back at mine,' Red
said as she scooped them all up. 'Come
on, we've got a secret meeting to attend.'

3

No ANYTHING!

apunzel and Ella sat on the floor of Red's tree house stuffing peanuts into their cheeks as fast as they could. Cole had managed to make them *look* human again, but a few hamster traits still remained.

'This is *so* embarrassing,' mumbled Rapunzel, shovelling in peanuts as she glared at the small blue fairy. 'I mean, *I'm* the royal princess! If anyone saw

24

me like this I'd be a laughing stock!'

'But *we've* seen you,' said Jack.

'You know what I mean,' said Rapunzel. 'Anyone *important*.'

Jack looked over at Red who raised one eyebrow.

'Don't worry, I'll fix it soon,' said Cole.

'Well, just as soon as you can would be good . . .' said Ella, spraying a mouthful of nuts all over the floor. Without hesitating she scooped them up and started stuffing them all back into her cheeks. Just then a small green monkey swung in through the door of the tree house and landed in front of them.

'Hey, guys!' said Alphege, stroking

his shiny green fur as he watched Ella and Rapunzel. 'Er, what's going on here?'

'Two words,' said Anansi. 'Well, three actually . . . *Cole and magic.*'

The monkey nodded. 'I *see* . . .' Alphege knew all about Cole's magic. It was after one of Cole's spells had

gone wrong that Alphege and his super-intelligent gorilla friends had first met the Tale Town gang – although it wasn't Cole's unpredictable fairy magic that made Alphege look like a small green monkey. *That* was a whole other story.

'What's the hurry?' he asked. 'Betsy

told me to "shift my furry green butt" – she can be *so* rude!'

Jack shuffled his feet awkwardly. 'She's probably just a bit tired – it puts her in a bad mood.'

'She's *always* in a –'

'– bad mood!' said Hansel and Gretel as they poked their heads up over the top of the ladder into the tree house.

Hansel and Gretel were twins who were so alike that they often finished each other's sentences.

'Yeah!' added Wolfie as he scampered up behind them, bringing with him the smell of coconut shampoo. 'She was *totally* mean to me just now. She told me to stop preening and get over here as soon as I could – but if I don't wash my tail with lavender water *and* blow dry it –' he wafted his tail around and the silky fur on it drifted gently through the air – 'it gets into the most *terrible* knots!' He sat down and adjusted his cap until it sat at *just* the right angle.

Wolfie was the Big Bad Wolf's son, but he was neither big *nor* bad – much to his dad's annoyance. The young wolf crossed his legs neatly and looked around at his friends. 'So, we're all here now. What's the mad rush?'

It wasn't long before everybody knew about the young troll prisoner and the friends had come up with a plan.

'And you're sure your gorilla friends will help?' asked Ella.

Alphege nodded his head. 'Absolutely! They'd do *anything* for me. I'm their King! Besides, I pay them *loads* of bananas each week . . .' He paused for a moment. 'Even if I didn't, I'm sure they'd still help.' He paused again. '*Probably.*'

Cole had finally managed to completely reverse his hamster spell, and after spitting out huge mouthfuls of peanuts, Ella and Rapunzel were busy describing what they had seen when they had sneaked into a troll festival a few weeks before.

'So . . .' said Jack thoughtfully when they had finished. 'The trolls were just wandering around, eating food, listening to music and selling goatskins and stuff? That just sounds like a normal festival.'

'*Exactly!*' said Ella. 'Trolls are just like us – I mean, sure, they got mad when they realized we were there, but before they saw us, they were all just having a nice time.'

'But what about that one that tried to eat me!' protested Alphege, '*He* didn't seem very nice.'

'Well, no . . .' agreed Ella. 'But remember that old woman who lived in the gingerbread house? She tried to fatten up Hansel and eat him?'

Everybody nodded.

'Well *she* wasn't very nice either, was she? You get good people and bad people – why would it be any different with trolls?'

'Good point.' Jack nodded. 'But even if our plan works and we manage to free the troll boy from the stocks, what then? Mayor Fitch's guards are all over the place – they'll catch him in no time.'

'Our camping trip!' exclaimed

Anansi suddenly, looking round at Red and Jack. 'My parents are taking us camping at the weekend – we can hide him away in one of the tent bags and he can come with us. Nobody will know *anything*! Well, not until we need to put up the tent.'

'That's settled then,' said Red. 'All we need now is a little bit of magic, and a lot of luck.'

'Oh that's no problem,' said Cole, 'I'll just—'

'*No!*' yelled Ella and Rapunzel at the same time.

'Thanks for the offer, Cole,' said Red. 'But maybe Jack should go and see Lily the Sea Witch for a spell – just *this* time. OK?'

The next morning, everything had been sorted out. The sun was rising on a clear fresh day as Hansel and Wolfie walked into the centre of Tale Town. The square was deserted apart from the young troll who was still in the stocks and three bored-looking guards. Wolfie carried a football under one arm as Hansel ran right up to a sign, which read:

NO BIKES or BALL GAMES

then yelled, 'Pass it over here, Wolfie!'

Wolfie made a good effort at kicking the ball to Hansel, but it sliced off at an angle and hit one of the guards square on the head. The guard glared at them, pointed at the sign with his sword and then jabbed the sword into the ball, which deflated with a hiss.

'Hey! That was my best ball!'

protested Hansel as the other guards laughed.

A moment later Gretel rode into the town square on a unicycle and wobbled around in front of the sign.

'Cut it out!' shouted the first guard, who was trying to dislodge Hansel's football from the end of his sword. 'Can't you read? No bikes!'

'It's not a bike,' said Gretel. 'It's a unicycle! So I can ride it wherever I like!'

Another guard, a burly woman with curly red hair, heaved herself up, headed over to the sign, pulled out a pot of paint and added:

or UNICYCLES!

at the bottom. Then she yanked Gretel's unicycle out from under her and threw it over a nearby fence.

'Hey!' protested Gretel, 'That's not fair!'

'Tough!' replied the guard.

That was when Ella came hopping past on a pogo stick.

'What are you playing at?' asked the guard crossly.

'Trying to see how many bounces I can do,' replied Ella, puffing.

'Seven thousand, three hundred and one, seven thousand, three hundred and two, seven thousa—'

'Stop it!' barked the red-haired guard. She added:

or POGO-STICK-ING

in squished writing to the sign, before swiping the pogo stick and bending it in two.

By the time Rapunzel had dragged her trampoline into the square and started jumping up and down while Alphege was practising juggling with some brightly coloured clubs, all three guards were furious.

'Get out of here!' shouted the guard

with the curly red hair. She crossed out the whole sign and changed it to read:

NO ANYTHING!

That was when one of Alphege's clubs *accidentally* flew out of his hand and bashed her on the nose.

'Get them!' roared the guard, running towards Alphege, who turned and sprinted off, closely followed by Rapunzel, Wolfie, Hansel, Gretel and Ella. The children were fast, but the guards were bigger and stronger, and it wasn't long before they had trapped the group against the bank of the river that ran through Tale Town.

'Got you!' shouted the red-haired guard.

There was a huge splash as Lily the Sea Witch burst up out of the river behind the group of children. Her eyes shone with magic and her long hair glistened like glass. She pulled the lid off a coloured jar and flung the contents of it all over the guards, who immediately crumpled and fell fast asleep.

'Did you see *that*?' she asked excitedly, looking at her friends. 'I mean, wow! Just *WOW*! Wasn't that *totally* fantabulous?'

Wolfie smiled. Lily was one of the most enthusiastic people he'd ever met. 'Sure was, Lily!' he said. 'Let's just hope everything else goes as smoothly.'

Alone in the town square, the troll child trapped in the stocks looked around nervously. Those children seemed to have led the guards away *on purpose*. As they ran off, the girl with the long blonde plaits had actually winked at him. *But why*? Why would *human* children try to help *him*?

There was a loud roar as a group of trolls burst into the town square. The prisoner's heart leaped. Finally he was being rescued! But how had they got past Tale Town's Moonstone defences? Moonstone stopped trolls being able to use their magic, and Tale Town was surrounded by it. The guards had even used Moonstone chains to secure the stocks. But it didn't seem to affect *these* trolls one bit.

That's when the young troll realized his rescuers weren't really trolls at all – they were *gorillas*, dressed up with masks on!

One of them held up a piece of paper with the words:

DON'T PANIC – WE'RE HERE TO HELP!

written neatly on it. Another gorilla snapped the chains, swung the troll boy up under one arm and then they all ran out of the square. As he bounced around under the gorilla's hairy arm, the troll boy could see that they were even wearing pretend troll feet as if they were shoes.

But why were they helping him at all?

4

The Campsite

*A*fter bouncing around for a few minutes the young troll found himself stuffed into a large canvas bag and put on the back of a cart. He poked his head out, but a girl with a bright red hood pushed his head down and gestured for him to be quiet. A second later, he heard her yell, 'Trolls! *Trolls!*'

The troll boy could hear the clanking sound of armed guards

running up towards the cart.

'They went *that* way!' said a boy's voice.

There was a small hole in the canvas bag, and the troll could just make out a human boy holding a bad-tempered hen pointing to what *looked* like a small group of trolls, running out of Tale Town. He had to admit, from this distance, the gorillas looked *very* convincing.

'We'll catch them!' called a guard. 'Don't you worry!' Then they were gone.

'What's happening?' whispered the young troll. The girl smiled as she passed him a bottle of water and a bag of snacks and then folded over the top of the canvas bag.

'We're going camping!' she replied.

'Shh!' said another boy's voice. 'My dad's coming!'

———◆◆———

It took a long time to get to the campsite. By the time the cart squeaked to a halt, everyone was relieved.

Anansi's dad, Mosi, ruffled his son's hair.

'This is where we're meeting your mum and uncle,' he said, 'They should be here any minute.'

'Great!' said Anansi as he climbed out of the cart with Jack and Red.

'**WhaAaaaat!**' squawked Betsy as she fluttered to the ground.

'We're *all* a bit stiff, Betsy,' said Jack.

'**Whaaaaat...**' said Betsy, looking upset.

'I *know* that you've got that old volleyball injury!' said Jack with a sigh. 'You *never* stop going on about it,' he added under his breath. 'Come on, we'd better get the tents up.'

'Good idea,' said Anansi's dad. 'Give me a second and I'll throw down the tent bags.' He climbed over the seats into the back of the cart and reached to pick up the bag that the troll boy was hidden in.

'*No!*' yelled Anansi, Red and Jack at the same time.

'Why not?' asked Anansi's dad with a frown. 'What's going on?'

'*Er . . .*' said Anansi, looking at Red.

'*Er . . .*' said Red, looking at Jack.

'*Er . . .*' said Jack, looking at Betsy.

Betsy shrugged and squawked, **'Whaʌaat?'**

Anansi's dad's mouth gaped open. 'Are you *seriously* telling me that we've just smuggled the escaped troll child out of Tale Town in a camping bag?'

Anansi, Red, Jack and Betsy nodded.

'Have you got *any idea* what would have happened if we'd been caught?' There was silence for a moment, before

Mosi added, 'Well, I can't say I blame you. Keeping a child locked up in those stocks – it just wasn't right.'

Anansi, Jack, Red and Betsy let out a sigh of relief as the tent bag wriggled and out popped the troll child's head.

'So . . . I guess I can come out now?' he asked with a shy smile.

———◆◆———

After he'd got over the shock, Anansi's dad had taken the news pretty well, and went off to feed the horse and put up the tents with Betsy.

'So your name is Quartzle?' Red asked the troll.

The troll boy nodded. 'But you can call me Quartz if you like.'

'Cool!' said Red. 'Well, I'm Red, this is Jack and this is Anansi.'

Both boys smiled and said hello.

'Look, it's not that I'm not grateful . . .' said Quartz slowly. 'But *why* did you help me? I know how much humans hate trolls.'

'Not *all* of us,' started Red, but she was distracted as two trolls burst into the clearing. Quartz froze in shock as Anansi leaped up and shouted, 'Rufaro! Mum! There you are!'

'*Mum?*' the troll boy said, his mouth hanging open. 'Your mum is a *troll?*'

Anansi laughed. 'Only in the daylight!' Then he ran over to give his mum a huge hug.

Quartz still looked confused so Red explained: 'Anansi's mum and uncle have been cursed by the troll warlock Hurrilan. They used to look like trolls all the time, but now it's only in the daylight. I guess that's why we're more used to being around trolls than some other people.'

'*Okaaaaaay . . .*' said Quartz slowly.

'So what happened?' asked Jack. 'How did Mayor Fitch's soldiers get you? It must have been *horrible*! Chained up in those stocks with no food or water . . . and what about going to the *toilet*?'

'Ahem! I think what Jack is trying to say . . .' said Red, elbowing Jack in the stomach and giving him a fierce look, 'is are you all right?'

'I am *now*!' said Quartz. 'Thanks to you and your friends!'

'Oh, it was nothing,' said Red, smiling.

'Well, it kind of was *something*!' said Jack. 'I mean, I spent HOURS making those troll feet . . .'

'*I. Was. Being. Polite!*' hissed Red under her breath.

'Oh. Right,' added Jack, smiling awkwardly. 'It was nothing. So anyway, what were you doing near Tale Town? It's pretty much the worst place to be a troll –  Mayor Fitch *hates* trolls!'

'I know,' replied Quartz. '*All* the trolls know. It was just last week that an army of his men came and set fire to my village.'

'What?' gasped Jack.

Quartz nodded. 'My village was just on the edge of the troll lands; pretty close to a few human villages, but everything always used to be fine . . . Then last week, some soldiers turned up and said that Mayor Fitch had decided our village was actually built on human land. I don't know why. Our village has been there for hundreds of years.'

'What happened next?' asked Anansi.

'What do you think?' said Quartz miserably. 'We're farmers, not fighters, and *they* had swords. They made us leave . . . and then a few hours later, all that was left of my village was ashes.'

'I'm so sorry!' said Anansi's dad as he walked over. 'That's just terrible!'

'We lost everything,' said Quartz sadly.

'**Whaaaaaat!**' squawked Betsy angrily.

Jack started to translate. 'She said that Mayor Fitch is a stupid, sausage-faced—'

'I know!' interrupted Quartz. 'I've no idea how I can understand her, but I do! Anyway, there's more. One of the guards stole an amulet we've had in my family for years. And I wasn't going to let them get away with *that*. So I sneaked out to follow them. I was trying to get it back when they caught me, and you know the rest. Now I've got *no idea* where my family are, or what I'm going to do.'

Red put her arm around Quartz's shoulders. 'Don't worry,' she said. 'We'll get you back to your family.' She looked around at her friends. 'Right?'

Anansi's uncle Rufaro nodded firmly. 'Absolutely! Fitch has gone *waaaay* too far this time. Let's all get a good night's sleep – we leave at first light.'

5

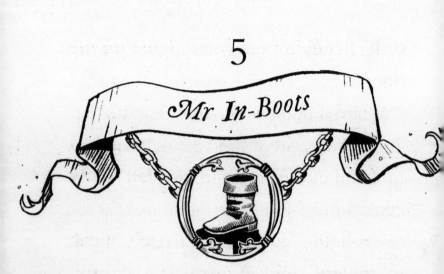

Mr In-Boots

*I*t turned out that first light was actually *really* early, and nobody was awake. Second light had long gone, and it was almost *third* light by the time Anansi peered out through the tent flaps to see his parents cooking breakfast while Rufaro packed up the cart.

'Morning, sleepyhead!' called Red who was sitting playing a card game with Quartz. 'How come you slept so well? I couldn't get comfy lying on the floor.'

'I had a hammock,' said Anansi.

'What?' protested Jack as he poked his head out of his tent. 'Not fair! How come I didn't get one?'

'Probably because you can't speak to spiders!' said Anansi with a grin. 'Thanks, guys,' he called to a group of spiders who nodded silently back at him and started taking down the hammock that they'd spun out of spider silk.

'Breakfast's ready!' called Adeola, Anansi's mum. 'Sausages and bacon! Come and get it!'

The children all rushed over to take their plates and sat down in a circle round the campfire.

'How about you, Quartz?' asked Jack through a mouthful of sausage. 'Did you sleep all right?'

'Yeah,' replied Quartz. 'Or at least I did at *first* . . .' He paused for a moment.

'Why?' asked Red. 'What happened?'

Quartz's eyes went wide. 'Well, I was lying there in my tent, when I suddenly heard this weird, rumbling, *growling*

sound. It got louder and *louder* and I got more and *more* scared until . . .'

'Until *what*?' asked Anansi breathlessly.

'Until I realized it was just *you* snoring!' said Quartz, and everyone burst out laughing.

'WhaAaaaaat!' said Betsy unusually seriously.

'You heard a rustling sound in the night when you needed the toilet?' asked Jack.

'It could have been *anything*,' said Red. 'But we should keep our eyes and ears open, just to be on the safe side.' She looked over at Quartz's plate which was piled high with fried tomatoes, eggs and beans but no sausages. 'So, how come you don't like sausages or bacon?' she asked.

'I just don't like to eat pigs,' replied Quartz.

'Seriously?' said Jack. 'But trolls eat goats! I mean, come on – that's gross!'

'Maybe, but humans eat pigs, cows, sheep *and* hens!' protested Quartz. 'Now *that's* gross!'

'WHAAAAAT!' squawked Betsy angrily.

'Exactly!' agreed Quartz and then turned back to Jack. 'I have a pet pig called Snout – Mum got her for me when I was little. She keeps my feet warm at night, and listens to my problems when I feel sad – how could *anyone* ever hurt a pig?' Quartz's eyes welled up a bit when he mentioned his home and family.

Red, Jack and Anansi looked awkwardly down at the sausages and bacon on their plates.

Jack slowly stopped chewing and swallowed everything in his mouth in one gulp before he put down his half-finished breakfast. 'Well, I'm full!' he exclaimed suddenly. 'Let's get everything packed up – the sooner we get going, the sooner we can find Quartz's family!

The cart was all packed, the horse was readied, and soon they were on the road. The first stop was going to be the site of Quartz's old village, so they could look for clues about where his parents and all the other trolls had gone. The only trouble was that they weren't sure how to find it.

They'd been travelling for about half a day when they saw a grumpy-looking cat wearing a pair of battered leather boots and a long tatty coat. They explained what Fitch had done to Quartz's village and asked if he knew where it was. The cat's hair was matted in clumps and his eyes were cunning and bright.

'Maybe I do, and maybe I don't,' he replied with a sly smile. 'What's it worth to you? I'll tell you this for nothing, though: if you're looking for that Fitch bloke, I knows a lot of folks round 'ere want a word with him. He's been causing a right old rumpus! He tried to take over the Marquis of Carabas's castle. Course, I sent 'im packing – ain't no one that can outsmart me! Anyway, I got places to be, know what I mean?' He winked and then swaggered off.

'So is he going to help us or not?' whispered Anansi.

'I don't know,' replied Red, 'but I

always thought Puss-in-Boots would be a bit more, you know . . . *charming*?'

'And a bit *less* grubby!' added Jack. 'He smelt like old cat food and bonfires!'

'What's that, sonny?' growled Puss from at least thirty metres away.

Jack looked at Red in a panic.

'Er, nothing . . . Mr In-Boots!' called Red. 'We were just talking about my, um, grandfather.'

'That may be,' growled Puss-in-Boots as he turned around menacingly. 'But remember this. I ain't the kind of kitty to play around . . .' He broke off, distracted by a bright beam of sunlight shining down on to the forest floor, and pounced on the light, trying to catch it with his paws.

'Wait a minute!' whispered Anansi. 'I've had an idea!' He rummaged around in the bags until he found a saucer and a bottle of milk. Then he clinked the bottle against the small plate. Puss-in-Boots looked up sharply and trotted over expectantly, his eyes locked on the milk bottle.

'Not so fast!' said Anansi with a smile. '*First*

you tell us where the troll village is.'

'Why, you sly old devil!' gasped Puss–in–Boots, then he winked. 'You remind me of myself at your age . . . Fair enough, it's a deal.'

While he was lapping up the milk, Puss told them exactly where the village was and how to get there. The children thanked him and the cart creaked off down the road. But *nobody* noticed the bushes rustling behind them as someone else ducked down out of view . . .

They travelled all day, making camp as evening fell and setting off again early the next morning. It was a long way to Quartz's village, and would take *ages* to get there.

Everywhere they went, they heard *more* stories about Mayor Fitch and how he'd been bullying people. It was the non-humans that he always seemed to pick on: talking trees, fairies, giants and dragons. None of them liked him, not even the super-friendly, rainbow-coloured unicorns from the Happy-Funshine Woodland – and they liked *everyone*.

The sun was low in the sky as they pulled up the cart and started to make camp for their second night on the road when out sprang a mean-faced little man with a short beard and pointy ears.

'*Found you I have, I knew that I would!*' he chanted in a sing-song voice which made everyone groan. '*Will you play my riddle? I think that you should!'* It was Rumplestiltskin.

'But we *know* what your riddle will be!' said Jack with a sigh. 'It's *always* the same!'

The little man smiled unpleasantly and twirled his beard between his fingers.

'Is that a no, or is that yes?

Answer me true, you must not guess!'

He paused and added in his normal voice. 'Actually, can you do me a favour and sign this contract first? I've been told that I need to make things more official – you know, health and safety gone mad!'

Red shook her head impatiently as she took the pen he was holding and signed the contract. 'OK, go on then. *Yes*, we'll play your riddle!'

Rumplestiltskin grinned.

'My riddle is this: You'll face no blame
If you can just tell me my name,
But if you can't, then you'll face strife,
As you will be my SLAVES FOR LIFE!'

Then he cackled, and capered and cartwheeled around, looking very pleased with himself.

'Your. Name. Is. RUMPLE-STILTSKIN!' shouted all the children together.

'No it's not!' replied Rumplestiltskin, bursting with fizzy excitement.

'Yes it *is*!' replied Red. 'You asked us the same riddle about three weeks ago!'

'I changed it!' cackled Rumple-stiltskin. '*Now* my name is *Nigel*, and you know what? It just feels *so* much more me!' He smiled happily. 'Anyway, now you're all my slaves for life! So to start off you can, let me see . . . carry me over to that comfortable-looking tree trunk, cook me dinner and then one of you can trim my toenails.' He peeled off one shoe to reveal the most gnarled, yellow and fungus-covered toenails that any of them had ever seen.

'**WhaAaaaaat!**' they all cried.

'I'm afraid so,' cackled the little man. 'Of course, if you'd guessed correctly, I'd have had to do *you* a favour – but you knew the deal.' He held up the contract Red had just signed, and pointed to the signature. 'So tough luck!' He jabbed Rufaro in the belly and said, 'Over to the tree trunk, if you please! I haven't got all day.'

Rufaro did *not* look happy.

'Wait!' called Red. 'If you're all *by the book* now, show me the document that *proves* you changed your name to Nigel!'

'I, er, don't have it on me. I dropped it earlier. In a river, by accident, and a fish ate it, then the fish got caught and cooked, so there's . . . um . . . no way you can see it now – sorry!'

'I don't believe you,' said Red, walking up so she was standing nose to nose with 'Nigel'. 'And *that* means *this* –' she snatched the contract out of his hands and ripped it up – 'doesn't mean *anything*!'

'Well, you can't blame me for trying!' protested Rumplestiltskin limply.

'I don't know . . .' said Rufaro crossly. 'I think I *definitely* blame you.'

Rumplestiltskin stared up at the tall, angry troll who towered above him.

'Look, no hard feelings? How about I do you a favour and then we call it quits?'

'OK!' said Red, her eyes lighting up. 'I know just what you can do. Have you got your spinning wheel?'

Rumplestiltskin nodded grumpily.

'Good!' replied Red as she looked round at her friends. 'Now we need to find as much straw as we can. Our good friend *Nigel* here is going to spin us a golden hot-air balloon. Right, *Nige*?'

6

A New Discovery

*B*ack in Tale Town, Ella, Rapunzel and Wolfie were looking in the window of a pop-up shop that had opened that morning. It only sold glass slippers, and you couldn't even get a pair. You had to buy one and then wait until someone with the *other* one wanted to come along and marry you.

'Glass slippers!' said Ella with a snort. 'Have you ever heard of a more ridiculous thing? Imagine how uncomfortable they'd be? What if they broke? Besides, who'd marry someone just because of the shoes they have?'

'Oh, I don't know,' said Wolfie, his nose pressed up against the window. '*I* think it's romantic . . .'

'We haven't heard from Red and the others yet,' Rapunzel interrupted with a worried frown. 'You'd have thought they'd have *some* news by now.'

'*Exactly*!' said Ella. 'But we've heard nothing! What if Fitch's men have got them? *Anything* could have happened!'

'I'm *sure* they're fine,' said Wolfie soothingly. 'They're probably still trying to find the troll boy's home, but even so, perhaps we should do a little –'

he lowered his voice – '*spying*? You know, see if Fitch *does* know anything? If we can get into his office without being seen, then we might find out something useful.'

'Great idea!' exclaimed Rapunzel. 'That sounds like a job for Hansel and Gretel.'

———◆———

As a patrol of Fitch's guards filed out of the Town Hall, none of them noticed the two dark figures that clung to the shadows behind them. That's because they were too busy noticing the noisy (but rather ineffective) fight that was happening between a scruffy young girl and a much neater young wolf.

'Help!' squealed Rapunzel, in her best *I'm-a-princess!-What-are-these-ruffians-up-to?* voice. 'They won't stop fighting!'

As the guards rushed over to break up Ella and Wolfie, Hansel and Gretel slipped out of the shadows and crept into the Town Hall.

One good thing about having been left on your own in the woods a lot is that you get extremely good at looking after yourself. Hansel and Gretel could hunt, climb, swim, run and do pretty much *anything* that they needed to do, silently and without anyone noticing. They could also communicate just by looking at each other, which was *very* handy on occasions like this.

Hansel twitched one eye slightly and waggled his left ear.

Gretel nodded. Of course it was going to be easy! All they had to do was get past Fitch's guards, sneak into his private office, find evidence of his evil plans and then get out again without being seen. She moved her jaw in a small side-to-side motion to say, 'And if we see any guards?'

Hansel narrowed his eyes, which Gretel knew could only mean: 'Sleep on sight!'

IT WASN'T LIKE THIS WHEN I WAS YOUNG!

Lily the Sea Witch had given them some tiny magic capsules containing the concentrated essence of '*It wasn't like this when I was young!*'. This powerful spell was made up of the complaints of older people, who were always moaning that '*It wasn't like this when I was young!*'. It was one of the most boring things you could ever hear and would make *anyone* fall asleep immediately.

Armed and ready to go,

with their blowpipes loaded with magic capsules, the twins tiptoed through the building towards Fitch's office. Five minutes later, having left a trail of sleeping guards behind them, they eased open the office door. No one was inside, so they slipped in to see what they could find. But there was nothing, apart from ordinary paperwork to do with the running of Tale Town. According to reports, sales of magic beans were down and a young girl with golden hair had been spotted breaking into people's houses, vandalizing their property and eating their breakfast. But there was nothing about the troll child at all.

Gretel scratched her chin to say: 'We

know Fitch is up to no good. Where does he keep all his private papers?'

Hansel blinked twice, meaning: 'Remember when we were here with Wolfie returning the Sacred Shiny Story-Snipping Shears and we found that secret cupboard? Let's look in there.'

Gretel nodded. Behind Fitch's desk was an ugly old painting. She gently tilted it to one side and a section of wall swung open, leading into a small chamber. Inside were the two sections of the 'Long Live the Story Tree' poem on stone slabs, just as they'd found them before – but nothing else.

Gretel frowned in disappointment and slumped heavily against a railing as Hansel crowded into the cupboard beside her. She screwed up her nose to say, 'There's *got* to be something else . . .' when with a sudden lurch the secret door swung shut behind them and the whole chamber began to sink into the floor.

Hansel looked over at Gretel with wide eyes that said, '*Uh-oh!*'

7

Deathrock-Skullgrind

'*Wow!*' exclaimed Red, peering down over the side of the golden basket that Rumplestiltskin had woven for them. 'I could get used to this!' The ground was rushing past hundreds of metres below as they floated through the sky, hanging beneath a golden hot-air balloon. As soon as Rumplestiltskin had finished the balloon, they had decided to travel on, and now the sun was setting, throwing a few last beams of pink light across the plains below.

'We're going so fast!' said Anansi. 'We must be well into the troll lands by now!' He looked over towards Rufaro. 'I can't believe that Rumplestiltskin was so helpful and told you which direction he'd seen all the trolls going in!'

Rufaro shrugged and looked a bit sheepish. 'Sometimes all you need to do is hold someone up in the air by their ankles and they become *very* helpful,' he muttered. 'Not that I advocate that sort of behaviour.'

'Look!' interrupted Quartz, pointing over towards some tall grey peaks in the distance. 'We're coming up to the Deathrock–Skullgrind mountains.'

'Seriously?' said Jack, going pale. 'That name doesn't sound too friendly . . .'

'Oh!' Quartz laughed. 'That's just how it sounds in troll language. Translated, it would mean '*Great towers of peace and beauty*'. Wait a minute! What's that down there?'

Everybody looked down to see long lines of trolls snaking towards the mountain range.

'It must be all the trolls from your village!' exclaimed Rufaro.

Quartz shook his head. 'There's too many – our village is only small.'

'Then who are all the others?' asked Anansi.

Quartz shrugged, but his eyes looked worried. The

last of the sun's rays disappeared behind the shadow of the mountains as the sky took on the cool tones of night-time.

'Fitch must have been attacking other vill—' began Rufaro, when a bright flash of magical light burst out from inside him. Seconds later, instead of being a big green troll, he had turned back into a human. Almost instantly there was another flash and Anansi's mum transformed as well.

'That *still* catches me by surprise!' said Anansi's dad. 'You'd have thought I'd have got used to it by now!'

'Wait a minute!' said Anansi. 'Did you hear that?'

'What?' asked Red.

'A sort of whistling, whooshing kind

of noise . . . There it was again! Listen closely . . .'

'Wait! I did hear it that time!' cried Red. 'It sounded a bit like an arrow flying past!'

'Yes!' agreed Anansi. 'It sounded *just* like that! And wait, did you hear that big boom too? The one that sounded kind of like a cannon?' He peered over the edge of the basket just as an arrow shot past one ear and a cannonball past the other.

'Yeaaaarrghh!' he yelled. 'We're being shot at!'

There are two main problems when you are being fired at while trapped in a small basket, hanging beneath a giant golden hot-air balloon. Firstly, you don't have anywhere to hide; and secondly, you're pretty easy to spot.

Soon the air was filled with arrows whistling up towards them.

'We've got to get out of here!' yelled Rufaro. 'It's only a matter of time before one of those arrows—' He was interrupted by a loud hissing sound as an arrow tore through the golden balloon. 'Hits us,' he finished unnecessarily.

More and more arrows ripped into the balloon. For almost a minute they struggled on, but then the balloon began to sink, slowly at first, and then faster

and faster until
they were tumbling
down towards the
mountains beneath them.

'Somebody *DO*
something!' shouted
Anansi's mum.
'We're going to
crash!'

'I can do
some magic!'
shouted
Quartz.

'Brilliant!'
replied
Rufaro.
'Can you
make the wind

blow up underneath us to slow us down?'

'Sorry,' said Quartz. 'I'm an earth troll. I could turn us all into stone?'

'I don't think that would help right now . . .' said Rufaro. 'But thank you anyway.'

'Whatever we do, we'd better do it soon!' shrieked Red. 'We're about to—'

◆

When the tiny chamber stopped moving, the wall in front of Hansel and Gretel opened again and the twins

found themselves looking out into a long, dimly lit room. It was completely empty, and there was no sound of anyone nearby. In the middle was a large table with some sort of model on it. Gretel looked over at her brother, who nodded. They both stepped out of the secret chamber, which immediately closed behind them and started rumbling back up to Fitch's office.

The model showed the whole of the Fairytale Kingdom, including the troll lands. In the centre of the troll lands was an enormous model of a mountain. There were a series of rings marked out in string over the model, with one final ring around the mountain itself. Evenly spaced around this last ring were models of twelve machines, all connected by a confusion of pipes and wires.

Hansel glanced at Gretel quizzically.

She raised one eyebrow to say, 'I have no idea either.'

A rumbling sound began behind them. The lift hidden in the secret cupboard was coming back!

As they looked around in panic, Gretel's arm knocked the mountain and it moved slightly. Her eyes lit up as she lifted the edge of it: it was completely hollow – they could hide *inside* it. They had just squeezed in when the door to the lift opened.

'Make sure you fire those guards!' exclaimed Mayor Fitch as he walked briskly into the room. 'Sleeping on the job indeed. I hope everything else is going according to plan?'

'Er, yes, sir,' replied another voice. 'We've been burning down *all* the troll villages near the borders. Thousands of trolls are making their way towards the mountains – it *must* be where the rebels are hiding.'

'And the machines?' asked Fitch. 'They're ready?'

'Absolutely, sir!' replied the voice. We just need to pinpoint the exact location of the troll warlock's secret base. We've sent spies out and they think that it could be either here . . .'

There was a puncturing sound as the end of a pin jabbed in through the mountain, spiking into Hansel's bottom.

'Mmph!' Hansel spluttered.

'Here . . .' continued the voice, as another sharp point jabbed through the model, poking into Gretel's shoulder.

'Eep!' she gulped.

'Or . . .' The voice paused. 'Sorry, I've run out of pointy flags – anyway, we think it's just *here*.' Hansel felt a finger tap the model of the mountain just between his eyes and breathed a sigh of relief.

'So . . .' said Fitch eagerly. 'As soon as we know we have the troll leader, we can activate the machines?'

'Indeed!' replied the other voice. 'They work perfectly! They strip the trolls of all their magical powers. They'll be like giant teddy bears, completely powerless!'

'Just imagine what we'll be able to do with all that magic!' exclaimed Fitch. '*Nobody* will be able to stop us!'

Gretel looked worriedly at Hansel.

He had a pained expression on his face. It could have just been because of the spike in his bottom, or it *could* have meant, 'You're wrong, Fitch! We're going to stop you!'

8

Marshmallow Mountain

*T*he horrible sound of seven people (and one hen) screaming in terror as they plummeted towards a rocky mountain was suddenly replaced by the shocked silence of seven people (and one hen) landing with soft *flumps* on the suddenly pink-and-white ground.

'Wait a minute,' said Red as she pulled herself out of the thick, sweet, soft, sticky surface. 'Is this mountain made out of . . . *marshmallow*?'

'Not usually!' came Quartz's muffled reply. He'd landed face first and only his feet were poking out of the soft, sweet ground. Rufaro and Anansi's dad heaved him out and he sat there for a moment, licking his lips. 'My earth magic can turn things into stone, *or* stone into other things,' he explained. 'So I just thought, what's the softest thing in the Fairytale Kingdom? And I was in a bit of a panic and came up with *marshmallow*.'

'Suits me!' exclaimed Jack, taking a huge bite out of the ground.

'Yeah, great work, Quartz!' said Red. 'You saved us all! Now all we

need to do is work out where the –
GIANT TWO-HEADED SNOW
LEOPARD!'

'What?' asked Anansi. 'Why on earth
would we want to find . . .' He trailed
off when he noticed that everybody
was staring directly behind him. Slowly
he turned around. '*GIANT TWO-
HEADED SNOW LEOPARD!*' he
yelped.

'Everyone stay *very* still!' whispered
Rufaro. 'What we need is to make
ourselves into a small—'

'*Icicles!*' shouted Quartz exuberantly.

'Er . . .' replied Rufaro. 'I was going
to say a small group, and *then* . . .'

But Quartz wasn't listening. He ran
towards the giant two-headed leopard

and flung his arms around both of its giant necks.

'*Icicles!*' he cried again. 'Aww, who's a good boy?'

'Sorry . . . Do you two know each other?' asked Anansi's mum.

'Sure we do!' said Quartz. 'Icicles is my dad's pet snow leopard. I've known him since he was tiny!'

The happy reunion was rather spoilt by the arrival of around thirty huge and heavily armed troll soldiers.

'Stay where you are!' bellowed their leader. 'Nobody move! Nobody even *think* about moving! Nobody even think about *thinking* about moving! Got it? Now, why were you flying over here? This mountain is out of bounds to humans!'

'Hold on a minute!' protested Quartz. 'They're not like the others – they *rescued* me! I was locked up in Tale Town until they saved me *and* they were trying to help me find my family! Which, I've got to say, is more than can be said for you! We could have died when our balloon crashed!'

The trolls looked at each other uneasily, and had a low, murmured conversation.

'All right!' said the leader. He pointed over to the torn remains of the balloon. 'Bring that back to base, and *you lot* –' he turned to face Red and the others – 'on your feet! There's someone who'll want to question you.'

'Can I ask who that is?' asked Rufaro politely.

'Sure,' replied the troll with a not-very friendly smile. 'It's our leader, Hurrilan. And he just *loves* humans!'

———◆———

Wolfie, Ella and Rapunzel had been hanging around outside the Town Hall for hours now.

'Well that's just *great*!' said Rapunzel. 'Now we've lost Hansel and Gretel too! How long have they been in there? Do you think something's gone wrong?'

Wolfie frowned. 'I'm not sure, but I'm fairly sure I can smell them.' He sniffed the air carefully. 'Hmm, yes, in this direction . . .' He started moving towards a rusty old drain cover. 'Yes, I'm getting definite hints of candy-cane mixed with a LOT of sewage.' He bent down close to the drain and added, 'Seriously, that smells *disgusting*!'

The cover of the drain wobbled, and Wolfie took a hurried step back as it slid out of place.

'You are *not* going to believe what Fitch is planning!' exclaimed Hansel as he poked his filthy head up out of the drain.

'Someone's *got* to stop him!' added Gretel, scrambling up behind him. 'He's gone completely *crazy*!'

'Yeah!' continued Hansel. 'Your parents are the King and Queen – right, Rapunzel? Surely *they* can do something?'

'But what's going on?' asked Ella. 'What did you find out? And why are you coming out of a *drain*?'

'We need to get to the palace and find Rapunzel's parents *now*!' said Gretel. 'We'll explain on the way!'

9

A Cold Night

*R*ed, Jack and the others were led
along a maze of narrow pathways
beneath huge mountain peaks that
scraped up towards the moonlit sky.
Flurries of snow swirled around them
and the air was so cold that Red could
see her breath billowing like smoke
from a dragon's snout.

It was not a pleasant walk and
nobody seemed to be enjoying it,

although Betsy and Icicles seemed to be getting on really well. She sat perched on his left neck, snuggling down into his shaggy white fur when she got too cold.

All of a sudden they turned a corner and the path ran into a huge, snow-covered plain, surrounded on all sides by tall cliffs which towered above them. The wide-open space was filled with tents and makeshift huts. Tired, thin-looking trolls peered out warily from the doorways or sat huddled around campfires which flickered in the cold night air. A few muttered angrily when they saw the humans and stepped forward to block their way.

'Calm down!' warned the soldier leading their procession. 'We'll have no trouble here!' He glared at the trolls in front of him and added, 'Unless you want to discuss it with Hurrilan?'

The trolls stepped aside, but continued to glare.

'But *we* haven't done anything wrong!' protested Red.

'Maybe not . . .' replied the troll that was leading them. 'But it's humans who've taken away their homes, their farms – *everything*. You can't blame them for feeling angry.'

They were led to a large tent in the middle of the plain and ushered inside.

'Wait here,' commanded the lead troll. 'I've set guards all around the tent . . . so don't bother even *trying* to escape.' He turned briskly and marched out.

'What do we do now?' whispered Anansi.

'There's not a lot we *can* do,' replied Rufaro anxiously. 'We just have to wait for Hurrilan . . .' He looked over at his sister. 'And I have no idea what he's going to say when he sees us!'

The tent flaps were flung back and all that could be seen in the sudden glare of a flaming torch outside was a tall, thin silhouette striding into the tent. 'Well . . . *look who it is!*' called out a voice. 'My dear old friends . . .' The words sounded friendly enough, but the voice was icy-cold. The tent flaps closed again and everyone could see Hurrilan's f a c e clearly.

He walked up close to Rufaro and Adeola. 'Admittedly, you look different to how I expected you would. You broke my curse? Impressive. But then again, if you can so easily break your promises – break a *friendship* – why wouldn't you be able to break a curse?'

'Look. I know you're angry . . .' began Rurafo slowly.

'Angry?' interrupted Hurrilan. 'When you and that boy *Fitch* –' he spat the word as though it was a bad taste in his mouth – 'tricked me into that cage all those years ago, you *broke* something in me! You were my best friends, my *only* friends! How could you do that to me? You'll never know how happy I was on the day my magic grew strong enough to track you down! And when my curse worked? Well, I felt as though – *finally* – I could let it all go! But here you are – back to taunt me! *Why?*'

'You've got it all wrong!' cried Anansi's mum. 'We were *never* friends with Fitch – he captured you to *hurt* Rufaro! I mean, he *does* hate the trolls, but he hates us just as much! After you escaped, he twisted everything so that our whole family had to leave Tale Town! We were banished and became outcasts – just like you . . .'

Hurrilan said nothing. His eyes darted between Rufaro and Adeola. Red, Jack,

Anansi and his father didn't dare move.

'So . . . he *lied*?' asked Hurrilan. 'You *weren't* trying to trap me?'

'No!' exclaimed Rufaro. 'Fitch has *always* lied – that's what he does!'

'You can prove this?' asked Hurrilan, his eyes narrowing.

'Well . . . he was very clever,' started Rufaro. 'He made sure that—'

'Yes!' interrupted Red. 'We can prove it!'

Hurrilan turned to face her, his cold eyes staring down.

'Well, I mean, you know . . .' stumbled Red. 'Maybe we can't prove exactly what happened when you were kids.

But Fitch has *definitely* been lying! We found the second half of the "Long Live the Story Tree" poem, which makes it clear that everyone should be allowed to use the Story Tree – even trolls!'

For a second Hurrilan stared at her, and then he laughed. Eventually he said, '*Even* trolls? It was a *troll* who wrote that poem! I suppose you didn't know *that*!'

Red, Jack, Anansi and all the others looked around at each other.

'But then again, why would you?' asked Hurrilan. 'That was hundreds of years ago. Before humans rewrote all the *old* stories with *their* version of events!'

'Seriously? A *troll* wrote "Long Live the Story Tree"?'

Hurrilan sighed. 'Is that *really* so hard to believe?' he asked. 'Anyway, you don't need to take *my* word. I can prove it!' He made a slight gesture with his fingers and a wooden chest appeared floating in the middle of the room.

'**Whaaaat?!**' croaked Betsy quietly.

'Yes,' said Hurrilan. 'I suppose it *is* rather impressive.'

The chest opened and Hurrilan pulled out a small, locked box. He took a key from his waist and slid it into the lock. The bolts and bars slid open one by one as the box opened to reveal a single, carefully preserved silver leaf.

'*This* is the oldest leaf from the Story Tree we still have,' he said. 'Hundreds of years old. Now, reach out *carefully*, and touch it – *then* you will see . . .'

Jack leaned forward, his heart pounding, and ever so gently, he touched the leaf.

10

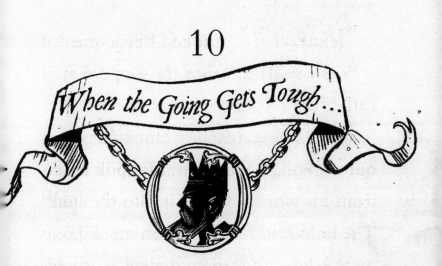

When the Going Gets Tough...

*A*s soon as Rapunzel had explained to her parents what they had seen in Fitch's secret war room, the King and Queen leaped into action. Well, that was *after* they'd finished having a massage and the cook had prepared their favourite lunch – a hot, fiery soufflé made out of phoenix eggs.

Then they had leaped into action.

Well, they agreed that the King should 'pop over to see what that confounded Fitch fellow was up to now'. 'Seriously, Dad!' protested Rapunzel as they walked towards the Town Hall, 'You've got to be careful! Fitch is *super-*clever!'

'Yes, yes, my dear,' replied her father. 'But is his so-called *cleverness* any match for my royal bearing, dignity and pride? I think *not*! I am the Crowned King among men! No, that ghastly little toad will have to just hop off, and *that* will be the end of *that*. The Fitch family have been meddling around here for too long. After all, I'm *the King*! Surely *I* should be the one making up all the rules! '

'But didn't you agree to the Mayor's office making all the "boring little decisions" about Tale Town so that you could have more holidays?' asked Rapunzel.

'Well, yes,' spluttered the King. 'But *now* I've decided it doesn't suit me. So I'm going to go into his office, find that second half of the Story Tree poem and show *everyone* the truth! Then he'll be gone and *everyone* will love me! I should have done it ages ago! Or at least, last month.'

'You were on holiday last month,' said Rapunzel.

'OK, well the month before *that*,' said the King.

'You and Mum were on a cruise.'

'Well, fine! It's not like *you* did anything to stop him, was it? Hmm? Little Miss *Know-it-all*!'

'Dad! I'm just a child! *You're* the King!'

'That's the trouble with today's youth!' muttered the King. 'No sense of responsibility! Anyway, let's get this done. My butler's running me a bath of warmed dragon milk and I *don't* want it to go cold.'

————— ♦ —————

Jack looked around in amazement. He was in the middle of Tale Town's square, but the Story Tree was far smaller, barely a sapling, and he only recognized one or two of the buildings. More surprising was that a crowd of trolls, humans, imps and other magical creatures were milling around happily together. In front of the crowd stood a man and a troll. They were standing side by side, wearing old-fashioned clothes and each holding up a giant stone tablet — one written in the trolls' language, and one in the humans'.

'My good friend Gravam has written this poem,' called out the man, 'so that we may all remember how lucky we are to have such a gift as the Story Tree in the town we have founded together!'

Everyone cheered.

Gravam smiled at his human friend and added, 'As long as we stay united, we can do anything! Long live the Story Tree! Long live Tale Town!'

The crowd went wild and repeated the chant. Jack had a few more seconds to look around, and then he was back in the tent with Red and the others.

***

'Whoa!' he exclaimed, looking up at Hurrilan in amazement, 'So trolls and humans founded Tale Town together?'

Hurrilan nodded.

'But why did it all change?' asked Anansi.

Hurrilan shrugged. 'Who knows?' he replied. 'But somewhere along the line it did, and things have been getting worse and *worse* for the trolls since then. At first we tried talking – but *nobody* listened. So now it's come to this, we're going to take what's ours. By *force* if we have to.'

'But don't you see?' said Rufaro. 'A war would be devastating! For both trolls *and* humans!

Look, I *know* that what Fitch has done is awful, I *know* that he needs to be stopped, but there has to be another way! The people of Tale Town are scared of trolls, but only because of what Fitch has told them. If we can stop Fitch, then we can make people see the *truth*!'

'And you'd help me do that?' asked Hurrilan.

'*Absolutely*,' replied Rufaro and his sister, Adeola.

The three old friends looked at each other for a long time. Then Hurrilan put a hand on each of their shoulders and quietly said, 'Thank you.'

11

A Victory (But for Who?)

'So you don't deny *any* of it?' asked the King as he stood in front of Mayor Fitch's desk. 'The hidden second half of the poem? The underground war room and the plan to enslave the trolls and steal all of their magic?'

Rapunzel, Ella, Wolfie, Hansel and Gretel were standing next to Rapunzel's dad. Everyone looked surprised.

'Not at all!' said Fitch cheerfully. 'I

suppose that's it, you win!'

'I do?' asked the King, looking confused.

'It certainly looks like it!'

'Yes, I rather suppose it does!' said the King, puffing up his chest. 'Now be a good fellow and fetch the second half of the poem, I need to show the townsfolk *immediately*. I'll be as lenient as I can, but it'll probably be the old "banishing to Far Far Away", I should imagine. No hard feelings?'

'None at all,' replied Fitch as he opened his secret cupboard and took out the stone into which the second half of the poem was carved. 'I'd have done *exactly* the same if things had been the other way around.'

'Right!' exclaimed the King, taking the stone. He couldn't quite believe that it had all gone so well. 'Well, I'll be off then. Come along, children.'

Rapunzel looked around as Mayor Fitch waved the King past, indicating that his guards should just let them all go.

'Something feels weird about this,' she muttered.

'Nonsense!' snorted the King, 'Fitch just knew better than to tangle with me! Now *come on*. I've got a town to save!'

The King strode to the door, opened it and walked out, before it suddenly slammed shut, trapping the children inside Fitch's office. He spun around, but his path was blocked by two of

Fitch's guards who had been waiting just outside the door.

'What's going on?' protested the King.

'Sir, we have reason to believe that you are in possession of stolen property,' said one of the guards loudly, as they grabbed the King by his elbows and dragged him out of the Town Hall.

'*What?* No! Listen, I can explain!' spluttered the King. He was making quite a commotion and a crowd was starting to gather in the town square. It wasn't every day you saw the King being held back by an armed guard.

'Oh? You can explain why you've been lying to us all these years?' asked Mayor Fitch as he strode calmly out of the Town Hall behind the King.

'*What?*' replied the King, confused, 'No! I was just—'

'Mark my words!' called out Mayor Fitch to the crowd, in his clearest speech-making voice. 'The King has been lying to *all of us*!'

There was a gasp from the steadily growing crowd as Fitch held up the original 'Story Tree' poem.

'We *all* know what this is!' he called. 'But do you see what *he* holds? There is *more* of the poem! A second half that we never even knew about!'

The King was indeed clutching the second half of the poem close to his chest – things weren't looking good.

'The royal family have been keeping us in the dark, all these years!' Fitch continued. 'There is a *secret* on that stone. A secret that the King wants to keep from us!'

'Boo!' shouted a voice from the crowd.

'Why?' yelled another.

'I don't know!' replied Fitch. 'Shall we find out?'

'*Yes!*' roared the crowd.

Fitch strode over to grab the stone. The King struggled to keep hold of it but Fitch wrenched it out of his hands, making sure that the stone fell as he did so. It tumbled down to the paving slabs beneath their feet and shattered into tiny pieces.

'What have you *done!*' exclaimed Fitch, sounding shocked.

'What do you mean?' replied the King. 'I didn't *do* anything, it was you who—'

'Friends!' shouted Fitch. 'For *years* the King and his family have lived a life of leisure! While you and I, the hard-working people of this town, sweat to put food on our plates!' Of course, this wasn't strictly true – the Mayor had *always* been paid very well – but the crowds weren't concerned about a detail like that right now.

'And *now* we find out he's been *lying* to us!' continued Fitch. 'What *else* has he lied about? Where does this web of deceit end? And what should we do with him?'

The crowd roared angrily, the King protested and Fitch stood there pretending to look as though he didn't know what to do next.

'My friends!' called Fitch finally, lowering his hands to calm the crowd. 'We have but one choice. The King, his family and supporters must be exiled! Sent to Far Far Away! Only *then* will we be safe from this treachery!'

The crowd roared its approval and Fitch nodded. 'Very well,' he said. 'We shall prepare the boat. They sail at dawn!' He gestured to the guards holding the baffled King. 'Secure the King, but make him comfortable. After all, he *is* royalty.'

Fitch waved one last time to the crowd, turned smartly on his heel and marched back into the Town Hall.

'Knock, knock,' he said, as he opened his office door.

Inside were Rapunzel, Wolfie,

Hansel and Gretel, who were tied up. Even though they hadn't been able to see what had happened to the King outside, they'd heard everything through the open window. Rapunzel's eyes were wide with panic.

'Don't worry,' Mayor Fitch said to Rapunzel in a low voice. 'You'll see him soon enough. You *all* will! After all, you're traitors too, and you'll be sailing off on that boat at dawn!' He laughed and then added, 'And don't think that your friends can help. My men have been following them since they left Tale Town with the troll child. Everything has worked out *even* better than I could have planned. They've led me *right* to where the troll warlock Hurrilan is hiding! I suppose I ought to thank you.' He smiled. 'I really couldn't have done *any* of this without you!'

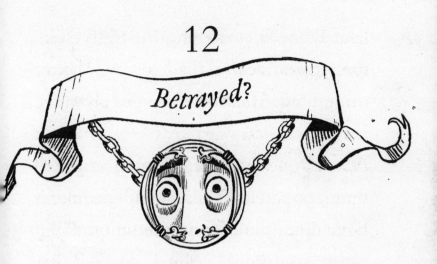

12

Betrayed?

'*I* am sorry, you know . . .' said Hurrilan as the children from Tale Town and Anansi's family all sat down to a troll banquet. 'For turning you into trolls? You see, I *really* thought that—'

'I know,' interrupted Rufaro, patting his childhood friend on the back. 'I understand. Although life *would* be a lot easier if you could completely lift the curse?'

'Of course!' said Hurrilan with a smile.

'But I'll need everything I used to make the original curse. As soon as I have everything to hand then I will. I promise.'

Quartz was sitting next to Red, Anansi and Jack after being reunited with his parents earlier that afternoon. Even Betsy had found the whole thing rather emotional. She'd covered her face with one wing and squawked a little **'WhAaaat?'** about having some dust in her eye.

Quartz's pet pig, Snout, Betsy, and Icicles the two-headed snow leopard were all in the corner eating from bowls on the floor. Betsy didn't look very happy about it – she *always* sat next to Jack at mealtimes.

They were halfway through dinner when one of Hurrilan's soldiers came in to announce that they'd fixed the hot-air balloon and it was being inflated outside, ready for their return to Tale Town. Now they had to work out how to get rid of Fitch and make sure that the trolls were once again allowed freely into Tale Town.

The royal ship, the *Silver Spoon*, was slowly pulling out of the Tale Town docks. Normally, when the boat pulled anchor, the harbourside would be lined with flag-waving townsfolk, keen to wish their royal family a happy journey.

NOT this time. Instead the crowd threw rotten eggs and mouldy cabbages. The King and Queen had run away sobbing to hide below decks.

Hansel and Gretel, their father and his newest wife were all on board too. As were Jack's family, Red's family, Wolfie, Rapunzel and Ella. The only person Fitch *hadn't* tried to round up was Wolfie's dad. Fitch might have been crazy, but he knew better than to try to mess with the Big Bad Wolf.

Jack's parents and Red's parents had fought and protested, scared their children would come home from their camping trip to empty homes, but Fitch had just sneered. 'They'll be following along in another boat, just as soon as they return from their so-called *camping trip*!' Then he had bundled all the adults into small servants' cabins, locked the doors and mounted guards outside.

Luckily for Hansel and Gretel, Rapunzel, Wolfie and Ella, they were allowed on deck as Fitch didn't see what harm they could do — after all, they were *only* children.

As the ship pulled out to sea, the

children looked sadly back towards Tale Town – *their home.*

'I can't believe it's ending like this!' said Rapunzel as she looked at the disappearing shoreline.

Ella put her hand on Rapunzel's shoulder. 'Don't worry. We'll come up with something. We *always* do!'

Rapunzel looked at her. 'Unless you think a giant octopus is going to reach its tentacles over the railings, put us all on its back and slip away from the ship without anyone noticing, then I *really* don't see how we're getting out of this!'

'**Whaaat...**' came a sudden sound from her left.

Rapunzel spun around, but there was nothing there.

'*Whoaaaaaah!*' came another noise from her right.

'What's going on?' cried Rapunzel as she turned around to see nothing again.

'I don't know!' replied Ella from behind her. 'Maybe it's a – *WAAAAAAAA!*'

'What's a *WAAAAAA*?' asked Rapunzel, turning around just in time to see a huge tentacle hoist Ella up into the air, over the ship's railings and then on to the back of a giant octopus, where Hansel, Gretel and Wolfie were balanced, looking very confused. Then a tentacle grabbed her too and she was whisked through the air towards the others.

'Sorry about the weird travel arrangements,' called Lily the Sea Witch from the water, 'but Ollie here

owed me
a favour,
and I
thought,
why not?
Right, Ollie?'
The giant
octopus stared
at Lily with
enormous expressionless
eyes and said nothing.

'He doesn't say much,'
added Lily. 'Still, he'll
get you all back to
shore, so hold tight!'

'But what about our
parents?' asked Rapunzel,
tying her long plaits into

149

a bow on top of her head so they didn't go anywhere near the salt water. 'They'll go *crazy* when they realize we're missing!'

'All taken care of!' replied Lily with a smile. 'A few seagulls owed me a favour too! Right now they're carrying notes up to the ship to be delivered to your parents. Now let's get you back to dry land!'

———— ◆ ————

The troll banquet was over and everyone was leaning back in their seats feeling happy and warm. The fire had been lit, and Hurrilan, Rufaro and Adeola were sharing stories about when they were young, while Icicles, Betsy and Snout dozed by the flames. Red looked around at all of her friends, old and new, and smiled.

'Hey, Quartz!' she said, tapping the troll boy on his shoulder. 'I'm really going to miss you when we go back to Tale Town! Promise you'll come and visit soon?'

'As soon as I can!' replied Quartz, 'But there's a lot of work to do before trolls will be accepted there.'

'I suppose so,' admitted Red sadly.

'But don't worry,' added Quartz. 'I've got this.' He dug down into his pockets and pulled out a small hand mirror. 'It's a magic mirror,' he explained. 'If you look into it while I'm looking into the other one, then we'll see each other in the reflection. Pretty cool, eh?

You can talk into it too!'

'*Really* cool!' exclaimed Red.

'So we can stay in touch, wherever we are!'

'I'd like that!' said Red happily as she took the mirror and gave her friend a warm hug.

They were interrupted by shouts and screams from outside and everyone leaped to their feet. A group of human soldiers ran in through the tent, carrying a lot of *very* unpleasant-looking weapons.

'My amulet!' gasped Quartz, pointing. One of the guards was wearing a stone carving around his neck that was shaped like a star: he ran straight up to Rufaro and said, 'Mayor Fitch will be pleased

with your work, Commander! You've
led us right to their hideout! Now come
on, let's get out of here!'

'*What?*' roared
Hurrilan and Rufaro,
staring at each other.

Hurrilan's face
crumpled in sadness
for a moment
before
immediately
hardening again.

'No,' protested
Rufaro. 'It's a trick!
I *swear* that—'

'Not again!' screamed
Hurrilan. 'How could I be so blind?
You led them here!' He picked up his

magical crystal-topped staff and swung it around above his head. The tent was plunged into darkness, then the crystal started glowing with a bright red light, leaving shimmering trails that twisted around each other, becoming almost solid. The light trails snaked through the air towards Rufaro and Adeola, twisting around them like a slow-motion lasso that bound them completely and dragged them back towards the glowing crystal.

'Stop!' yelled Anansi. 'Leave them *alone*!' He ran forward but Hurrilan flicked his hand and

Anansi shot backwards against the wall of the tent, unable to move.

'That must be him!' yelled the soldier with the amulet, pointing at Hurrilan. '*Get him!*'

The soldiers all ran towards Hurrilan, but he effortlessly cast another spell sending them tumbling backwards, turning into goats as they fell. The amulet flew into the air and Jack leaped up to catch it.

'Hurrilan!' gasped Rufaro as he was dragged closer to the crystal. 'It's a trick . . . I swear!' The snaking lines of light were fizzing and spitting with magical energy, and Rufaro and Adeola were shrinking in size as they neared the powerfully glowing stone. 'They're lying!' finished Rufaro's voice, in barely more than a whisper, as the light dimmed and was sucked back into the crystal – taking Rufaro and Anansi's mum with it.

'No!' shouted Anansi at Hurrilan.

'What have you done? We didn't know anything about it! I promise!'

'It's too late,' said Hurrilan, glaring at Anansi and the others. 'You've ruined everything. Now there is *nowhere* that trolls are safe. We can't stay here – and it's all *your* fault! Why would you do this?'

At that moment, one of the frantic soldiers Hurrilan had turned into a goat ran into the troll warlock, knocking him off balance and making him drop his staff. As Hurrilan bent over to pick it up, Quartz gave him a quick nudge from behind and he fell forward. Another goat picked up the staff in its teeth and Hurrilan scrambled up to chase after it.

'Quick!' whispered Quartz to the rest

of the group. 'Get out of here! Now!'

'But what about my mum and Rufaro?' asked Anansi.

'You can't do anything about that now!' said Quartz's dad. 'You *must* leave!'

'He's right!' said Anansi's dad. 'It's not safe. I need to get you and the others to the hot-air balloon.'

Jack pressed the amulet into Quartz's hand and scooped Betsy up. They all scrambled out of the tent and ran towards the golden balloon. Although it was patched and battered, it looked like it could still fly. They leaped inside and rushed to throw the weighted sandbags over the side, but for some reason, the balloon only rose a few feet into the air.

'Oh no! We forgot to untie the guy-ropes!' cried Anansi's dad.

The scared group of humans (and one hen) peered over the side of the basket. A sea of angry troll faces surrounded them, coming closer with every second.

Jack heard an arrow flying towards them and instinctively ducked. But instead of piercing the balloon, the arrow sliced through one of the guy-ropes holding the balloon down. A second arrow sliced through another rope and then with a loud *shhhhwipppp* another cut the last remaining rope and the basket rose into the air.

Red looked down at the mass of angry trolls beneath them. In among them she saw Quartz and his parents,

holding their
bows and making
the smallest
possible waves
as Hurrilan
finally caught
up with the
goat and snatched
his staff back.

'You'll pay!' he yelled up at
the balloon as it rose past the
mountain peaks and out of
range of his magic.
'This is just the
beginning!'

SHHHWIPPP!

13

Home Again

The journey back to Tale Town was fast, but that was the only good thing anyone could say about it.

Anansi barely said a word, and sat slumped in the corner of the basket with his dad sitting next to him. 'What happened to Mum and Rufaro?' he asked, his voice shaking. 'Are they all right?'

'I'm sure they are,' replied his dad. 'I don't know how, but I just have a feeling. I'm going to find somewhere safe for you all in Tale Town and then I'm going back! I'll find them – I promise.'

'But *nowhere* will be safe in Tale Town!' protested Red. 'Fitch's men must have been following us the whole time! We can't go back!'

'I know *somewhere* that will be safe!' said Jack, his eyes lighting up.

'WHAAAAAAAAT!?!' squawked Betsy excitedly.

'Exactly!' said Jack. 'Rufaro's secret hideout! If it's good enough for Alphege and the gorillas, then it's good enough for us. We can *all* camp there together!'

'That's *perfect*!' said Red. 'We can be close enough to Tale Town to keep an eye on what Fitch is up to, but he won't know that we're there.'

'OK,' agreed Anansi's dad. 'Let's wait until nightfall, then we can land in the Wild Woods without anyone finding out.'

———◆———

Late that night, after the hot-air balloon had been deflated, folded up and hidden away, Red, Jack, Betsy, Anansi and his dad crept through the woods towards Rufaro's secret hideout. As they closed in, Jack thought he saw a light shining through the trees, but it went out almost immediately.

'Did you see that?' he whispered. 'I think there's someone there!'

Red's face was pale. 'OK,' she replied. 'We'll go the long way round and sneak up, just to be on the safe side.'

They crept through the grass as quietly as mice. Well, as quietly as huge loud mice . . .

Eventually they came to the hideout. Jack tiptoed out into the clearing and was whipped off his feet, dangling upside down in a particularly ingenious trap. Alphege and the gorillas leaped out of hiding, along with Ella, Rapunzel, Wolfie, Hansel and Gretel. When they realized it was Jack they all burst out laughing.

'We thought you were one of Fitch's guards!' exclaimed Rapunzel.

'We thought *you* were!' replied Red with a grin.

'No way!' cried Hansel and Gretel

together. 'It's so good to see you guys again!'

'Yeah! You too!' said Anansi.

'*Helloooooo!*' called Jack from far above their heads.

'So what brought you here?' asked Ella excitedly.

'Same as you, I guess,' replied Anansi. 'We needed somewhere safe to hide.'

'Well, come in, come in!' exclaimed Wolfie. 'I've been trying to make things a *bit* more comfortable. I've woven a couple of rugs and found some scented candles . . . well, I say *scented*, I think they're scented with earwax – they smell *vile!*'

'Er, they *are* earwax,' replied Anansi. 'Rufaro had a bit of an ear problem last week . . .'

Wolfie looked as though he was going to be sick.

'That all sounds *great*,' interrupted Jack as he swung back and forth above them. 'But can you please *get me down*?'

One of the gorillas lowered Jack slowly down to the floor and Alphege got the campfire going again. 'OK, so gather round, people!' he exclaimed happily. 'We've got some tinned pasta shapes to eat, and a *lot* of stories to tell!

By the time the embers of the fire were fading, everyone was ready for bed. Red, Jack and Anansi had told everyone about the trolls' secret mountain. Rapunzel had explained about Fitch banishing the King and Queen, and Hansel and Gretel had told the story about Fitch's secret war room.

Then Alphege explained how they'd popped in to see one of the gorilla's aunts for the afternoon and had ended up staying for a few days, going for long walks and eating lots of blackberry crumble and custard.

'Oh!' said Red. 'Well . . . that sounds nice. I mean, the rest of us have been having all these dangerous adventures, and it turns out that you guys were just hanging out?'

Professor Hendricks – whose aunt they had visited – picked up a stick to write a few words in the ground:

IT'S IMPORTANT TO RELAX!

'I suppose so,' said Red with a shrug.

'Anyway, what are we going to do now?' asked Rapunzel.

Red looked around at her friends and smiled. 'We're going to take back Tale Town!' she said firmly. 'We're going to get rid of Fitch, and then we're taking *back* our town! And we'll make sure the town welcomes everyone. Humans *and* trolls.'

The End . . . (or is it?)

Quartz

Strengths: Brave, kind, loyal and generally good-natured

Weaknesses: He gets a bit grouchy when he's hungry – who doesn't, right?

Likes: His new friends in Tale Town, and bringing trolls and humans together

Dislikes: Mayor Fitch

Old Bert

Strengths: A super-humanly bad sense of smell. Which might not seem like a strength – unless you were around rotten fish all day

Weaknesses: He's not *quite*★ as sneaky as he'd like to think he is. ★*Nowhere near!*

Likes: Fish. Just fish

Dislikes: Lily-livered landlubbers who have never done an honest day's swindling in their lives!

Mayor Fitch

Strengths:	Cunning. Lying. Cheating. Being mean and, surprisingly enough, making pretty little origami birds – but that's just a hobby
Weaknesses:	He doesn't have any real friends, just people who are afraid of him
Likes:	See strengths
Dislikes:	Trolls. All Trolls

Puss-in-Boots

Strengths:	Very clever and knowledgeable about all sorts of different things
Weaknesses:	Rather lacking in social graces. He can seem a touch rough around the edges
Likes:	Milk. Ideally a milk-flavoured biscuit on top of milky ice cream in a frozen-milk bowl with a side order of milk
Dislikes:	Bathing. Water. And, worst of all, bathing in water